SCOOBY-DOO!
OVER THE BOARDWALK

PAUL KUPPERBERG ★ WRITER
FÁBIO LAGUNA ★ ARTIST
HEROIC AGE ★ COLORIST
TRAVIS LANHAM ★ LETTERER
VINCENT DEPORTER ★ COVER
HARVEY RICHARDS ★ EDITOR

Spotlight

visit us at www.abdopublishing.com

Reinforced library bound edition published in 2013 by Spotlight, a division of the ABDO Group, PO Box 398166, Minneapolis, MN 55439. Spotlight produces high-quality reinforced library bound editions for schools and libraries. Published by agreement with Warner Bros.-A Time Warner Company.

Printed in the United States of America, North Mankato, Minnesota.
102012
012013

♻ This book contains at least 10% recycled materials.

Library of Congress Cataloging-in-Publication Data

Kupperberg, Paul.
 Scooby-Doo in Over the boardwalk / writer, Paul Kupperberg ; artist, Fabio Laguna. -- Reinforced library bound edition.
    pages cm. -- (Scooby-Doo graphic novels)
 ISBN 978-1-61479-052-5
1. Graphic novels. I. Laguna, Fabio, illustrator. II. Scooby-Doo (Television program) III. Title. IV. Title: Over the boardwalk.
 PZ7.7.K87Sck 2013
 741.5'973--dc23

                    2012033326

All Spotlight books are reinforced library bindings and manufactured in the United States of America.

SCOOBY-DOO!

Table of Contents

OVER THE BOARDWALK

PAUL KUPPERBERG ★ WRITER   FABIO LAGUNA ★ ARTIST   HEROIC AGE ★ COLORIST
TRAVIS LANHAM ★ LETTERER   VINCENT DEPORTER ★ COVER   HARVEY RICHARDS ★ EDITOR

BUT THEY'RE *WRONG...* IT'S THOSE APARTMENT BUILDINGS THAT ARE A DANGER TO ONE OF BROOKLYN'S GREAT *HISTORIC* AREAS!

I AGREE WITH *YOU.* I... HUH?

≥Gasp!≤ IT... IT'S *BACK...* AND LOOKING AS *REAL* AS BEFORE...!

IT'S NOT...IT *CAN'T* BE!

OH, I *KNOW!* THE QUESTION IS, *WHO* IS CREATING SUCH A *CONVINCING* FAKE...?

MEANWHILE, ON THE BOARDWALK...

RMMMM!

CANDY APPLES

YOU SAID IT, PAL! I, LIKE, *LOVE* COTTON CANDY...

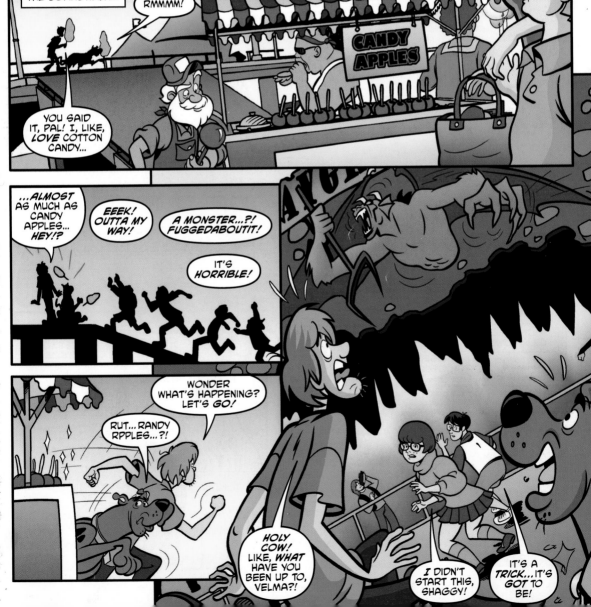

...ALMOST AS MUCH AS CANDY APPLES... HEY!?

EEEK! OUTTA MY WAY!

A MONSTER...?! FUGGEDABOUTIT!

IT'S HORRIBLE!

WONDER WHAT'S HAPPENING? LET'S *GO!*

RUT... RANDY RPPLES...?!

HOLY COW! LIKE, *WHAT* HAVE YOU BEEN UP TO, VELMA?!

I DIDN'T START THIS, SHAGGY!

IT'S A *TRICK...*IT'S GOT TO BE!

DID I JUST HEAR SOMEONE...?

≈SOB!≈

I *THOUGHT* SO! HELLO? ARE YOU ALL RIGHT...?

NO... I... I NEED *HELP*...!

JINKIES! WHAT HAPPENED TO YOU, LADY?

I... I'VE BEEN *POISONED*...

OHMIGOSH! LET ME CALL AN *AMBULANCE*...!

NO! NO DOCTORS... THERE'S *NO TIME!* BESIDES-- THERE'S *NOTHING* THEY CAN DO FOR ME!

I WAS POISONED BY MY UNCLE WHEN HE FOUND OUT I'D LEARNED OF HIS PLAN TO KILL MY MOTHER AND SEIZE CONTROL OF THE FAMILY CHEMICAL COMPANY!

UNCLE HOWARD IS A *BRILLIANT* CHEMIST... HE INVENTED AN *UNDETECTABLE* POISON TO KILL HER WITH...

...BUT HE USED IT ON *ME* FIRST! I... I HAVE TO *FIND* HIM BEFORE HE HURTS MOTHER... AND GET THE *ANTIDOTE* BEFORE IT'S *TOO LATE* FOR ME...!

LADY, DID *YOU* BUMP INTO THE *RIGHT* STRANGER! *TAXI!!*

CITY BUS

TAXI

WHATEVER IT IS, I HOPE IT HELPS YOU *SOLVE* IT...!

GOOD AFTERNOON, MISS SALLY! I'M SORRY, BUT YOUR MOTHER'S NOT HERE! SHE LEFT A LITTLE WHILE AGO...

...TO MEET YOUR UNCLE IN THE CITY FOR DINNER! SHE DIDN'T SAY *WHERE*...

≷GASP!≷ *OH, NO!* I...I HOPE WE'RE NOT *TOO LATE!* COME ON...WE CAN USE ONE OF MOM'S CARS!

I'M RIGHT BEHIND YOU, SALLY!

AND, SHORTLY...

THANKS FOR DRIVING, VELMA! TH-THE *DIZZY* SPELLS ARE GETTING *WORSE*...

...AS THE POISON SLOWLY KILLS ME...BUT WE... WE *MUST* WARN MY MOTHER...

WHEN YOU CALLED HOWARD'S OFFICE, THEY DIDN'T KNOW *WHERE* HE HAD GONE. IS THAT USUAL?

NO...JUST THE *OPPOSITE!* UNCLE HOWARD *ALWAYS* STICKS TO A VERY *STRICT* SCHEDULE!

I WISH MOM WASN'T ALWAYS FORGETTING TO *CHARGE* HER *CELL PHONE*...THERE'S NO WAY TO GET IN TOUCH WITH HER!

WE NEED TO KNOW *WHERE* THEY'RE MEETING! MAYBE WE CAN CATCH UP WITH UNCLE HOWARD--

"--*BEFORE* HE LEAVES TO MEET YOUR MOTHER!"

...SORRY, MISS GERBER, BUT YOUR UNCLE'S ALREADY *LEFT* FOR THE EVENING!

¿GROAN!¿ THERE'S OUR *LAST* CHANCE TO FIND HIM...!

NOT SO *FAST!* DO YOU HAVE A KEY TO HIS APARTMENT...?

HE GAVE ME ONE *YEARS* AGO, IN CASE OF AN *EMERGENCY!* BUT THE DOORMAN WILL *NEVER* LET US UP IF HOWARD'S NOT THERE!

YOU JUST KEEP THE DOORMAN *BUSY* AND LEAVE THE *REST* TO ME...!

THAT-A-GIRL! DISTRACT HIM FOR JUST A *SECOND*...

...AND MR. DOORMAN NEVER NEEDS TO KNOW ANYONE'S SLIPPED PAST HIM!

NORMALLY, I'D NEVER BREAK INTO SOMEBODY'S APARTMENT LIKE THIS...

...BUT WE'RE RUNNING *OUT* OF TIME TO STOP *TWO* MURDERS!

SALLY SAID HER UNCLE ALWAYS KEEPS TO A *STRICT* SCHEDULE, SO I'M BETTING THAT EVEN IF HE DIDN'T TELL HIS *OFFICE* WHERE HE WAS GOING--

--HE *STILL* WROTE IT DOWN *SOMEWHERE!*

AH-HAH!

IT'S *BLANK*...NO-- *WAIT!* HE TOOK THE PAGE HE WROTE ON WITH HIM...

...BUT THE *PRESSURE* OF THE *PENCIL* LEFT AN *IMPRESSION* OF WHAT HE WROTE ON THE PAGE *UNDERNEATH!*

IF I RUB THE *SIDE* OF THE PENCIL *LIGHTLY* OVER THE PAGE, IT SHOULD *REVEAL...* AH!

"6:30 CCC"! THAT'S OBVIOUSLY A *TIME*...BUT *WHAT--* OR *WHERE--*IS "CCC"?!

I'VE LOOKED *EVERYWHERE*... AND I *STILL* DON'T HAVE ANY IDEA WHAT "CCC" MEANS...!

≈Whew!≈ SALLY SURE WASN'T *KIDDING* WHEN SHE SAID HER UNCLE WAS A *CHOCO-HOLIC...!*

MOMENTS LATER...

...AND IF YOU'LL MAKE SURE MY UNCLE GETS THIS MESSAGE, I'LL BE...

ER... *THERE* YOU ARE, SALLY! SORRY, I, UH... THOUGHT YOU WENT INSIDE!

HUH?!

THANKS, MR. DOORMAN! SEE YOU LATER...!

QUICK, SALLY! WHERE'S THE NEAREST LIBRARY?! I'VE GOT TO DO SOME *RESEARCH*!

CRAZY KIDS...

SHORTLY...

...*CLOSED!!* WE'RE *TOO* LATE! *WHERE* AM I GOING TO FIND THE BOOK I NEED AT *THIS* HOUR...?

CITY LIBRARY

THE *BOOKSTORE!* IT'S STILL OPEN!

SALLY, YOU'RE A *GENIUS...!*

I JUST NEED A MINUTE TO... TO...

BURNS & NORBEL'S MEGA-SUPER-BOOKSTORE

MYSTERY WRITER CAL MELVIN CULLINS!

STRANGE CASE OF THE ONE-FOOTED MAN

MYSTERY WRITER CAL MELVIN CULLINS!

THE STRANGE CASE OF THE POISONED PIE

WHAT IS IT, VELMA? WHAT'S WRONG?

THOSE *MYSTERY NOVELS...* BY CAL MELVIN CULLINS--*THAT'S* WHY THIS CASE SOUNDED SO *FAMILIAR* TO ME!!